THIS BOOK BELONGS TO

....

HANSEL AND GRETEL

Written by Helen Anderton

Illustrated by Stuart Lynch

make
believe
ideas

Reading together

This book is designed to be fun for children who are learning to read. The simple sentences avoid abbreviations and are written in the present tense. The big type also helps children with their word-shape recognition.

Take some time to discuss the story with your child. Here are some ways you can help your child take those first steps in reading:

※ Encourage your child to look at the pictures and talk about what is happening in the story.

※ Help your child to find familiar words.

※ Ask your child to read and repeat each short sentence.

※ Try using some of the following questions as you go along:
  • What do you think will happen next?
  • Do you like this character?
  • What kind of voice would this character have?

Sound out the words

Encourage your child to sound out the letters in any words he or she doesn't know. Look at the key words listed at the back of the book and see which of them your child can find on each page.

Reading activities

The **What happens next?** activity encourages your child to retell the story and point to the mixed-up pictures in the right order.

The **Rhyming words** activity takes six words from the story and asks your child to read and find other words that rhyme with them.

The **Key words** pages provide practice with common words used in the context of the book. Read the sentences with your child and encourage him or her to make up more sentences using the key words listed around the border.

A **Picture dictionary** page asks children to focus closely on nine words from the story. Encourage your child to look carefully at each word, cover it with his or her hand, write it on a separate piece of paper, and finally, check it!

Do not complete all the activities at once – doing one each time you read will ensure that your child continues to enjoy the story and the time you are spending together. Have fun!

Hansel and Gretel
live with their dad
and stepmother, Clare.

They only
have brown
bread to eat.

Clare says to Dad, "We are too poor to feed the children. They must leave!"

Clare leads them into the woods. Gretel leaves a trail of crumbs.

Clare runs away.
The children look for
the crumbs. But birds
have eaten them.

Hansel is very scared.
Gretel hugs him.

But then they see a house.
It is made out of treats!

13

They eat the house!
They munch on the
roof and the door.

15

A witch comes out and Hansel screams!

"My house is ruined!" says the witch.

The witch looks at her house. She feels very sad.

The children feel bad.
The witch is not scary.

Hansel and Gretel
draw a plan to
fix the house.

The children lick and
munch. They turn the
house into a castle!

The witch is pleased.
She waves her
wand to add cream!

Hansel, Gretel, and
the witch live happily
in their new home.

What happens next?

Some of the pictures from the story have been mixed up! Can you retell the story and point to each picture in the correct order?

Rhyming words

Read the words in the middle of each group and point to the other words that rhyme with them.

dream

scream

cream

thing

will

feet

green

treat

sweet

teeth

bird

crunch

munch

lunch

wall

can

plan

girl

man

woods

floor

witch

hitch

stitch

was

floor

door

house

poor

wall

Now choose a word and make up a rhyming chant!

The witch **screams,**
"I **dream** of **cream!**"

Key words

These sentences use common words to describe the story. Read the sentences and then make up new sentences for the other words in the border.

The family is poor.

Clare takes the children **to** the woods.

They leave crumbs behind them.

They **see** birds eat the crumbs.

Hansel **is** scared.

like · very

· his · but · see · with · all · we · asked · was · go · her

Hansel and Gretel see the house **made** of treats.

They eat the house.

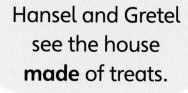

The witch feels **very** sad.

They make a new house **for** her.

They **all** make friends.

Picture dictionary

Look carefully at the pictures and the words.
Now cover the words, one at a time.
Can you remember how to write them?

bird

bread

castle

cream

door

roof

stepmother

treats

witch